ST
THE

What Would
Captain
Picard
Do?

by Brandon T. Snider

Penguin Young Readers Licenses
An Imprint of Penguin Random House

PENGUIN YOUNG READERS LICENSES
An Imprint of Penguin Random House LLC

TM & © 2017 CBS Studios Inc. STAR TREK and related marks are trademarks of
CBS Studios Inc. All rights reserved. Published by Penguin Young Readers Licenses,
an imprint of Penguin Random House LLC, 345 Hudson Street, New York, New York 10014.
Manufactured in China.

ISBN 9780515157147   10 9 8 7 6 5 4 3 2 1

Use caution when traversing the vastness of space. Such a magnificently complex system is sure to hold unexpected mysteries and curious dangers.

Pay attention—
the galaxy is full of surprises.

Never follow orders indiscriminately. Trust in your superiors, but if they should ever present a morally questionable request, challenge them on it. It is your *duty*. Blind obedience is the tool of monarchs and madmen.

IT HAS NO PLACE IN A FORWARD-THINKING SOCIETY.

Negotiation can be a tricky beast.

If you anticipate a testy exchange of ideas with an obstinate entity, bring along a healthy dose of patience and perhaps a sturdy commander or two. This will show your adversary you mean business.

WHEN YOUR CREW NEEDS YOU,

Should your crew become frenzied, losing
control of their emotions and becoming
difficult to lead, remember that they are not
themselves. They've been infected with a
bizarre and mysterious illness that has
plagued the universe for centuries. It will
pass, and when it does, make sure they rest.

Doctor's orders.

The Arabian horse—what a magnificent creature.

The weight of command seems
to drift away when one is in the soothing
presence of such a majestic beast. Recreation
is a valuable tool that allows us to take leave of
the mundane aspects of our lives and truly
appreciate the beauty that surrounds us.
It can be quite empowering.

Do not surrender when confronted by a creature comprised of pure, titanic inhumanity, no matter how noxious and repugnant it may be. Confront it with its own loneliness.

Show the creature its flaws, and it will cry out with a red rage the likes of which you've never heard.

The Borg believe that perfection can be achieved by assimilation. One might expect this kind of flawed logic from artificial intelligence. Mankind, however, has hope on its side.

Let freedom, individuality, and self-determination prevail.
Resist with every fiber of your being.

Building relationships can be difficult if you're a meek individual. Using the holodeck for a bit of playacting can help loosen you up and build confidence. But never let such a thing get in the way of your duties.

Fantasy and reality must be kept separate.

Even the most experienced leaders make mistakes.

To assume a commanding officer will escape them is a fallacy. What a remarkably cocksure mindset, and a silly one at that. Studying one's missteps is important, but always remember to *expect the unexpected.*

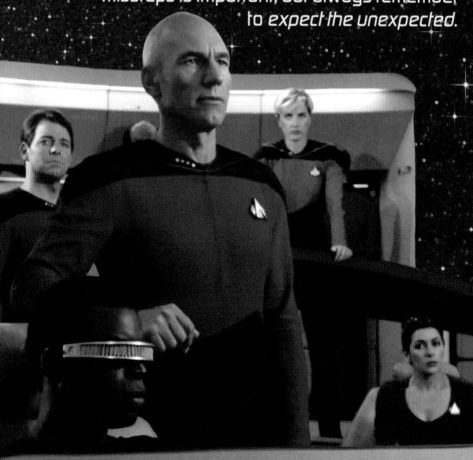

**Anger will consume you
if you let it.**

For all intents and purposes,
it's a healthy human emotion,
but people become blinded
by anger, turning them
into school yard bullies.
If you find yourself in a state
of acrimony, work through
your outrage.

Get to the other side.

Once the madness has lifted,
use the remaining energy to
focus on the problem at hand.

You might as well use it for
something productive.

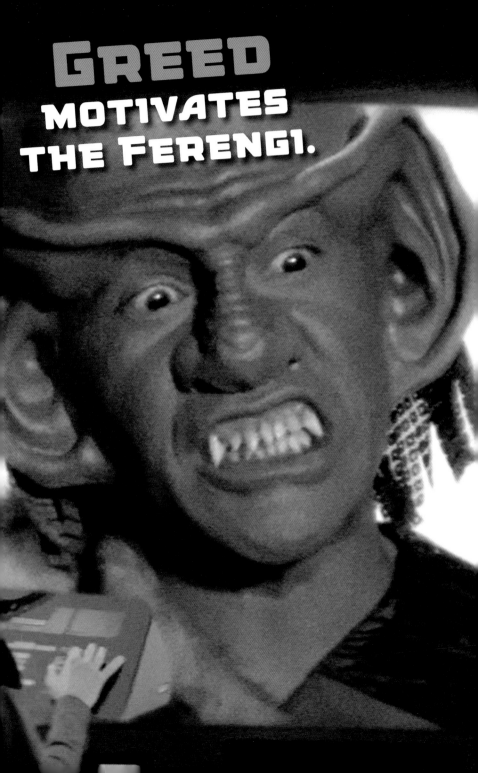

GREED MOTIVATES THE FERENGI.

It clouds their judgment and drives them to commit unspeakable acts of deception, and even violence. Be wary. They make negotiation difficult, and an encounter with them can leave you with quite a headache . . . though that could just be their thought maker brainwashing you.

MAINTAIN YOUR WITS, AND CONTINUE TO MONITOR THE SITUATION.

Scientific inquiry is the cornerstone of civilization.

A simple mind may look at a person's outward appearance for signs of villainy. Such an approach would be a grave mistake. True evil is an affliction. To find its core, one must go much deeper.

Think critically and carefully when assessing the physical aspects of others.

Judging a book by its **cover** does not serve mankind well.

When things seem dire,

don't forget to engage in a bit of fun.

The *transporter room* is no place for hijinks.

A professional workplace must be maintained for the good of the crew. Horseplay should be kept to recreational areas *only*. A commander is loath to reiterate such basic rules, but crew behavior dictates that it *must be done*.

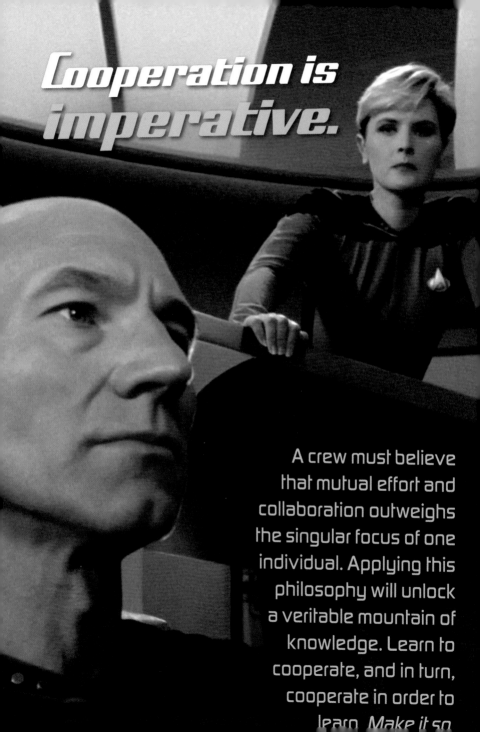

Cooperation is imperative.

A crew must believe that mutual effort and collaboration outweighs the singular focus of one individual. Applying this philosophy will unlock a veritable mountain of knowledge. Learn to cooperate, and in turn, cooperate in order to learn. *Make it so.*

Have faith in your junior officers.

They've trained diligently to fulfill their purpose and must be given the room to do so, especially when you and your crew are in danger.

If you're rendered unable to lead, trust that you've taught your junior officers well.

Let them lead the way.

It is inevitable that you will find yourself trapped: in traffic, in long meetings, or perhaps even by a band of kidnappers. While it may seem like you are surrendering to the situation in silence, you always have control of your thoughts, and you can use this time to let your mind explore the possibilities of your escape and what to be thankful for once you are free.

When dealing with an ill crew member, be sure to conduct a thorough assessment. Check for changes in appearance and behavior. You never know when an alien virus may be incubating inside them, lying in wait, readying itself to decimate worlds.

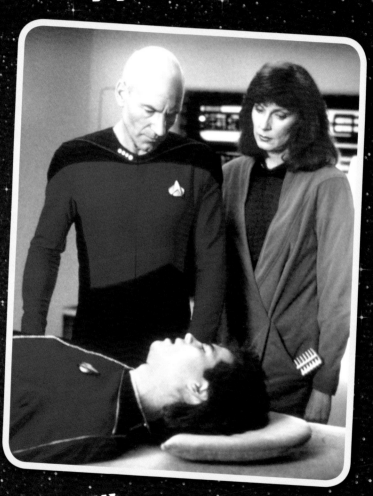

To borrow a phrase— ***stay vigilant.***

Dealing with an omnipotent being who can bend time and space can be exhausting. Such a thing requires more patience and fortitude than you can imagine. Summon these traits from within the depths of your soul and cling to hope.

Unless you're dealing with the likes of Q, **then all bets are off.**

Temporal disruptions can cause a host of bizarre effects.

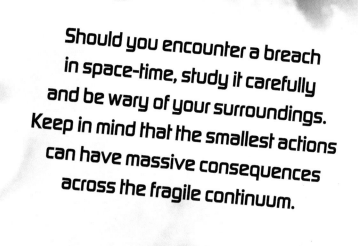

Should you encounter a breach in space-time, study it carefully and be wary of your surroundings. Keep in mind that the smallest actions can have massive consequences across the fragile continuum.

Be cautious when approaching infinity.

You needn't explore the depths of the galaxy or possess a holodeck to get lost in a good mystery.

A STURDY DETECTIVE NOVEL DOES THE TRICK QUITE NICELY.

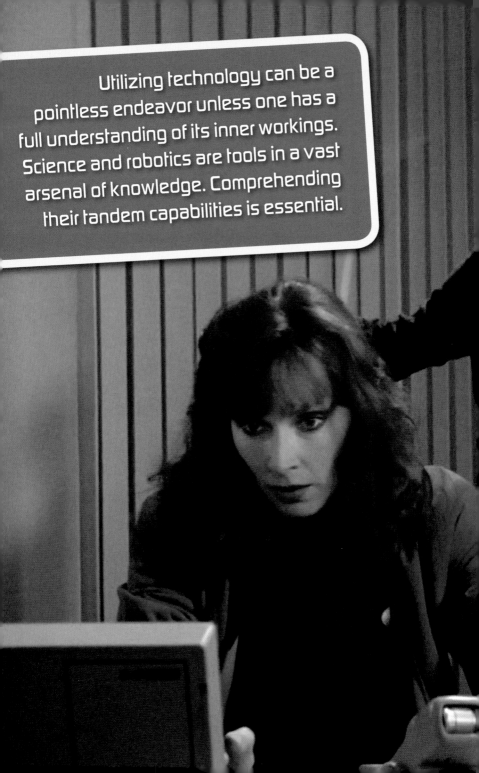

Utilizing technology can be a pointless endeavor unless one has a full understanding of its inner workings. Science and robotics are tools in a vast arsenal of knowledge. Comprehending their tandem capabilities is essential.

Don't take innovation for granted.

Dealing with incessant matters of life and death can be overwhelming for anyone. Command can often produce intense anxiety, but don't let stress consume you. Speak to a colleague or medical professional should you feel as if you're losing clarity of thought. Anything else is simply not worth the risk.

When an alien race that feasts on the neural energy of humans makes a desperate leap through time in order to secure nourishment, remain calm. Should a logical and reasoned appeal fail you, a precise photon torpedo strike may prevent further incursions.

One hopes.

The desire for material possessions is not uncommon; however, to value *things* above *people* is absurd.

Baubles mean nothing in a society that does not champion the oppressed. Put your energies into raising up those without a voice instead of acquiring trinkets. It will fulfill you in ways you've never imagined.

LISTEN TO THE CONCERNS OF YOUR CREW.

Make yourself available for private as well as group discussion. Accessibility is pivotal to command, and when a crew feels understood, they do their best work.

It also prevents conspiracy.

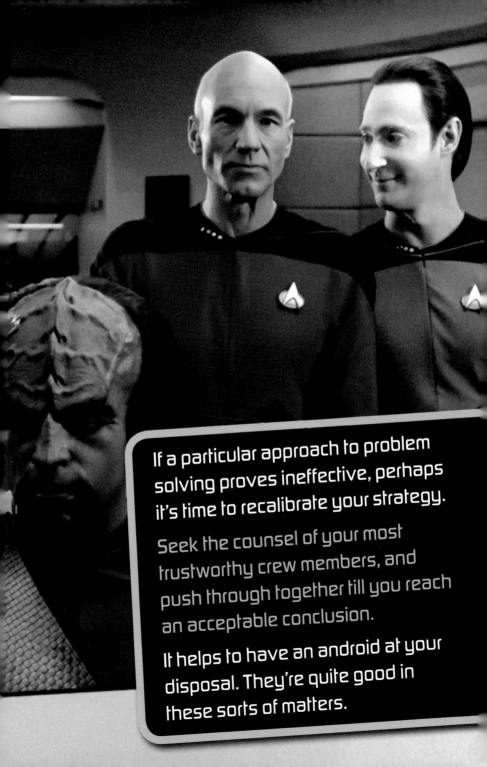

If a particular approach to problem solving proves ineffective, perhaps it's time to recalibrate your strategy.

Seek the counsel of your most trustworthy crew members, and push through together till you reach an acceptable conclusion.

It helps to have an android at your disposal. They're quite good in these sorts of matters.

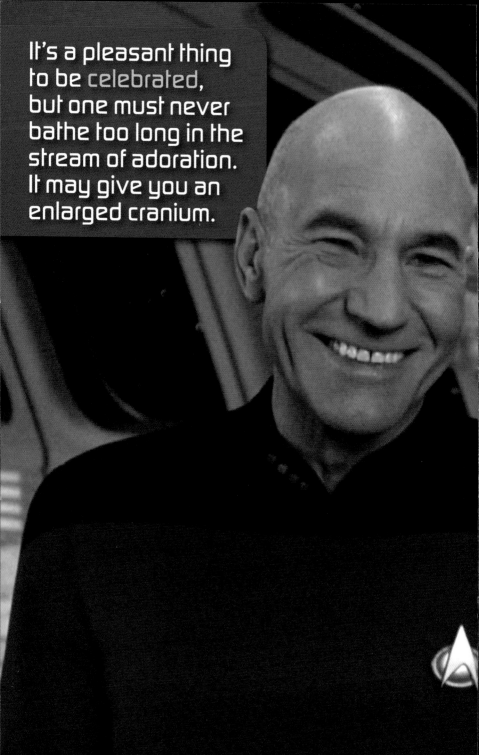

It's a pleasant thing to be celebrated, but one must never bathe too long in the stream of adoration. It may give you an enlarged cranium.

Accept the honor and move on. There's work to be done, after all.

Temporal rifts have the capacity to change time lines and throw reality into chaos. *Preparedness is critical.* Thoroughly assess your surroundings, paying careful attention to shifts and inconsistencies. Alert your crew to stay vigilant. Frankly, it's impossible to be prepared for everything, but that doesn't mean you shouldn't try.

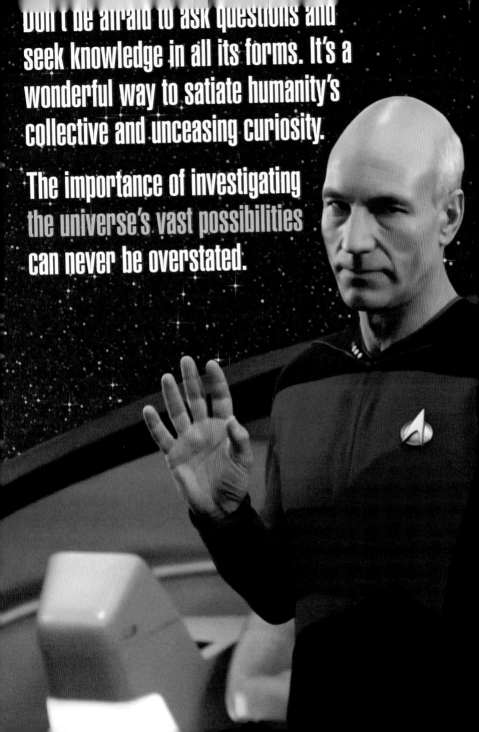

Don't be afraid to ask questions and seek knowledge in all its forms. It's a wonderful way to satiate humanity's collective and unceasing curiosity.

The importance of investigating the universe's vast possibilities can never be overstated.

Worship can be
an uncomfortable sensation.

Humans are not gods and should not be glorified as such. Remember the Prime Directive. Should you discover a primitive civilization that believes you to be divine in nature, taking advantage of this would violate your most important oath. Tread very carefully going forward. The healthy development of their civilization depends on your actions.

The Ressikan flute can be an incredibly relaxing instrument . . . especially after you've experienced a lifelike simulation observing the death of a civilization over the span of forty years. Learning to master a musical instrument is one of life's most wonderful joys.

Don't wait until the *death of civilization* to discover your *hidden talent.*

Leadership is a taxing station. Handling intergalactic business takes its toll. Find time for a warm cup of Earl Grey tea when you can. It'll settle your mind. The rich citrus flavor may even excite your taste buds.

Take pleasure in life's minute thrills.

If a Betazoid diplomat invites you to dinner, make sure you wear your finest Starfleet uniform.

Looking the part is a prerequisite for diplomacy and command.

Always dress and comport yourself properly and with authority.

Be forewarned—you may be more irresistible than you realize. If this is the case, take a deep cleansing breath and use your best judgment.

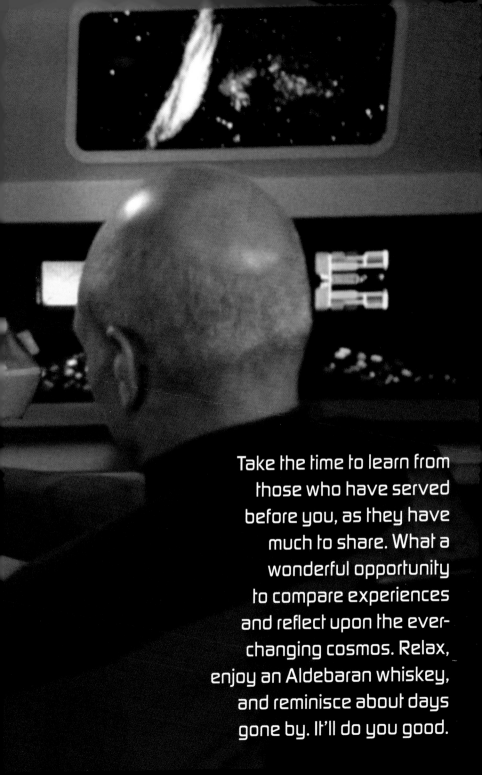

Take the time to learn from those who have served before you, as they have much to share. What a wonderful opportunity to compare experiences and reflect upon the ever-changing cosmos. Relax, enjoy an Aldebaran whiskey, and reminisce about days gone by. It'll do you good.

What a surreal sensation to encounter a future version of yourself.

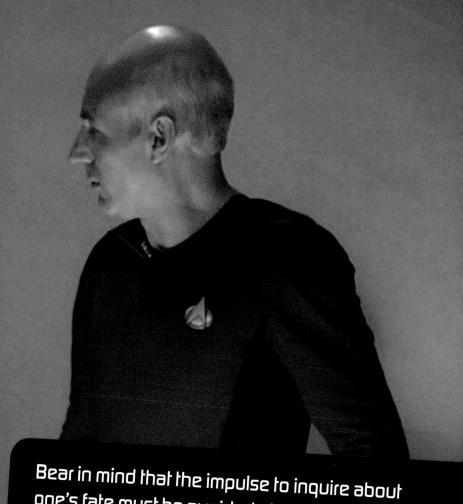

Bear in mind that the impulse to inquire about one's fate must be avoided at all costs. Doing so may rupture the time stream. Of course, if your own doppelgänger stands before you, the time stream may be ruptured regardless. Temporal mechanics can be a very complicated business.

Should a medical treatment accidentally infect your crew and devolve them into prehistoric beasts, *do not panic.* Simply seek out the amniotic fluid of a nearby pregnant woman and concoct a hasty antidote. *Good luck.*

Stepping into the shoes of someone else allows one to experience a new perspective.

It can also be quite enjoyable under certain circumstances.

Control
is merely an
illusion.

EMBRACE LIFE!

What are you waiting for?

Live now!

Make now always the most precious time.

Now will never come again.

I don't recommend making vulgarities part of one's daily vocabulary, but a smartly used Klingon curse word can make all the difference during a challenging situation.

It also feels good to say
"baQa'!"

Despite its unappealing nature, arranged marriage has been used as a diplomatic tool for eons. Love and affection are distasteful bargaining chips, but an empathic metamorph has a duty to fulfill their purpose, no matter the personal cost. Don't fall in love with one, either.

It will save you some heartache.

Practical jokes *can be a humorous and unexpected salve when the rigors of command weigh heavy upon your breast.*

life's
curiosities!

When your spirit hails you,

open a channel.

What is death? Is it an ending or another state of being? A formless immortal named Nagilum questioned these notions, threatening to destroy the crew of the *Enterprise* for sport. It ultimately concluded that humanity was too militant for its tastes.

Ah, the *irony*.

Listening
is the
backbone
of
communication.

The enigmatic El-Aurians can receive and interpret audible information with great precision and care. They're remarkable listeners. If you're feeling anxious, it helps to speak to someone.

We are all on this journey called life *together.*

Consider all the angles.

We've all done regrettable things in our youth.
The key is to acknowledge such choices, learn
from them, and move on. They are all threads
in the tapestry of your life. Why bother with
a past you cannot change?

It's crucial that one maintains a sense of mental well-being when on a mission.

Not just for yourself, but for the prosperity of your crew as well. Speak with one of Starfleet's exceptionally trained counselors to help relieve the pressures of service. Deanna Troi, for example, is an expert psychologist, a keen empath, and a superb listener. Utilize the expertise of your crew and the skilled professionals around you.

Commander William T. Riker is an exemplary officer.

He possesses the fantastic ability to find unorthodox solutions when every other plausible option has been exhausted. It's impressive. He's also damn good with the trombone.

Seek out someone close to you who has your back and make them your Number One.

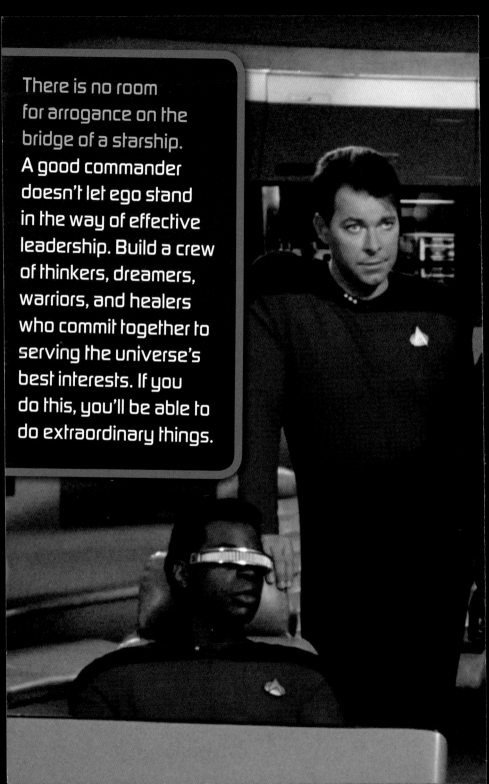

There is no room for arrogance on the bridge of a starship. A good commander doesn't let ego stand in the way of effective leadership. Build a crew of thinkers, dreamers, warriors, and healers who commit together to serving the universe's best interests. If you do this, you'll be able to do extraordinary things.

Within all of us is the raw potential to rise above our meager beginnings and excel beyond the stars. Remain determined against all odds and stay the course.

The dream of a bright future is within your grasp—*you need only reach out and touch it.*